The Night
Before
Christmas

The Night Before Christmas

A Visit from St. Nicholas

By Clement C. Moore ❈ Illustrated by Tom Browning

STERLING INNOVATION
An imprint of Sterling Publishing Co., Inc.

New York / London
www.sterlingpublishing.com/kids

STERLING, the Sterling logo, STERLING INNOVATION, and the Sterling Innovation
logo are registered trademarks of Sterling Publishing Co., Inc.

10 9 8 7 6 5 4 3 2 1
05/09

Published by Sterling Publishing Co., Inc.
387 Park Avenue South, New York, NY 10016
© 2009 by Sterling Publishing Co., Inc.

Illustrations © 2009 by Tom Browning

Distributed in Canada by Sterling Publishing
c/o Canadian Manda Group, 165 Dufferin Street
Toronto, Ontario, Canada M6K 3H6
Distributed in the United Kingdom by GMC Distribution Services
Castle Place, 166 High Street, Lewes, East Sussex, England BN7 1XU
Distributed in Australia by Capricorn Link (Australia) Pty. Ltd.
P.O. Box 704, Windsor, NSW 2756, Australia

Sterling ISBN 978-1-4027-5484-5

For information about custom editions, special sales, premium and
corporate purchases, please contact Sterling Special Sales
Department at 800-805-5489 or specialsales@sterlingpublishing.com.

Introduction

Amid the many Christmas Eve traditions, held in various places by different persons, there was one in New York City not like any other anywhere. A company of men, women, and children would gather together just after the evening service in their church, stand around the tomb of Dr. Clement C. Moore, the author of "A Visit from St. Nicholas," and recite together the words of the poem which we all know so well and love so dearly.

Dr. Moore was born in a house near Chelsea Square, New York City, in 1781, and he lived there all his life. It was a great big house with fireplaces in it—just the house to be living in on Christmas Eve.

Dr. Moore had children. He liked writing poetry and wrote a whole book of poems for them. One year he wrote this poem, which we usually call "'Twas the Night before Christmas," to give to his children as a Christmas present. They read it just after they had hung up their stockings over one of the big fireplaces in their house. Afterward, they learned it and sometimes recited it, just as other children learn it and recite it now.

It was printed in a newspaper, then a magazine printed it, and after a time it was printed in the school readers. Later it was printed by itself, with pictures. Then it was translated into German, French, and many other languages. It was even made into "Braille," which is the raised printing that blind children read with their fingers. So it has happened that almost all the children in the world have read this poem!

'Twas the night before Christmas,

When all through the house

Not a creature was stirring,

Not even a mouse;

The stockings were hung
  By the chimney with care,
In hopes that St. Nicholas
  Soon would be there.

The children were nestled
All snug in their beds,
While visions of sugarplums
Danced in their heads;

And Mamma in her kerchief,

And I in my cap,

Had just settled our brains

For a long winter's nap,

When out on the lawn

    There arose such a clatter,

I sprang from the bed

    To see what was the matter.

Away to the window

I flew like a flash,

Tore open the shutters

And threw up the sash.

The moon on the breast
    Of the new fallen snow
Gave the luster of midday
    To objects below,

When, what to my wondering eyes
    Should appear,
But a miniature sleigh,
    And eight tiny reindeer,

With a little old driver,

So lively and quick,

I knew in a moment

It must be St. Nick.

More rapid than eagles
His coursers they came,
And he whistled, and shouted,
And called them by name,

"Now, Dasher! Now, Dancer!

Now, Prancer and Vixen!

On, Comet! On, Cupid!

On, Donder and Blitzen!

To the top of the porch!
To the top of the wall!
Now dash away! Dash away!
Dash away all!"

As dry leaves that before

The wild hurricane fly,

When they meet with an obstacle,

Mount to the sky;

So up to the housetop
The coursers they flew,
With the sleigh full of toys,
And St. Nicholas too.

And then in a twinkling,
I heard on the roof
The prancing and pawing
Of each little hoof.

As I drew in my head
And was turning around,
Down the chimney St. Nicholas
Came with a bound.

He was dressed all in fur,

From his head to his foot,

And his clothes were all tarnished

With ashes and soot;

A bundle of toys
    He had flung on his back,
And he looked like a peddler
Just opening his pack.

His eyes, how they twinkled!
His dimples, how merry!
His cheeks were like roses,
His nose like a cherry!

His droll little mouth

 Was drawn up like a bow,

And the beard of his chin

 Was as white as the snow!

The stump of a pipe

     He held tight in his teeth,

And the smoke, it encircled

     His head like a wreath.

He had a broad face

And a little round belly,

That shook when he laughed,

Like a bowlful of jelly.

He was chubby and plump,

A right jolly old elf,

And I laughed when I saw him,

In spite of myself.

A wink of his eye

And a twist of his head,

Soon gave me to know

I had nothing to dread.

He spoke not a word,

But went straight to his work,

And filled all the stockings,

Then turned with a jerk,

And laying his finger

Aside of his nose,

And giving a nod,

Up the chimney he rose.

He sprang to his sleigh,

To his team gave a whistle,

And away they all flew,

Like the down of a thistle.

But I heard him exclaim,

As he drove out of sight,

Merry Christmas to all,

And to all a good night!"

The End